Date: 5/16/23 Staff initials ICB /FRM

Tag!
&
In Pip's Bag

Early ★ Reader

First American edition published in 2020 by Lerner Publishing Group, Inc.

An original concept by Jill Atkins
Copyright © 2020 Jill Atkins

Illustrated by Julia Seal

First published by Maverick Arts Publishing Limited

Licensed Edition
Tag! & In Pip's Bag

For the avoidance of doubt, pursuant to Chapter 4 of the Copyright, Designs and Patents Act of 1988, the proprietor asserts the moral right of the Author to be identified as the author of the Work; and asserts the moral right of the Author to be identified as the illustrator of the Work.

All US rights reserved. No part of this book may be reproduced, stored in a retrieval system, or transmitted in any form or by any means—electronic, mechanical, photocopying, recording, or otherwise—without the prior written permission of Lerner Publishing Group, Inc., except for the inclusion of brief quotations in an acknowledged review.

Lerner Publications Company
An imprint of Lerner Publishing Group, Inc.
241 First Avenue North
Minneapolis, MN 55401 USA

For reading levels and more information, look up this title at www.lernerbooks.com.

Main body text set in Mikado. Typeface provided by HVD Fonts.

Library of Congress Cataloging-in-Publication Data

Names: Atkins, Jill (Children's author), author. | Seal, Julia, illustrator. | Atkins, Jill
    (Children's author). Tag! | Atkins, Jill (Children's author). In Pip's bag.
Title: Tag! ; & In Pip's bag / by Jill Atkins ; illustrated by Julia Seal.
Description: Minneapolis : Lerner Publications, [2020] | Series: Early bird readers.
    Pink (Early bird stories) | "An original concept by Jill Atkins." | Originally
    published in Horsham, West Sussex by Maverick Arts Publishing Ltd in 2018.
Identifiers: LCCN 2019008643 | ISBN 9781541578043 (lb : alk. paper)
    ISBN 978-1-5415-8283-5 (EB pdf) | ISBN 978-1-5415-7805-0 (lib. bdg.)
    ISBN 978-1-5415-8727-4 (pb : alk. paper)
Subjects: LCSH: Readers (Primary)
Classification: LCC PE1119 .A796 2020 | DDC 428.6/2—dc23

LC record available at https://lccn.loc.gov/2019008643

Manufactured in the United States of America
1-46881-47785-4/26/2019

Tag!
&
In Pip's Bag

Jill Atkins

Illustrated by
Julia Seal

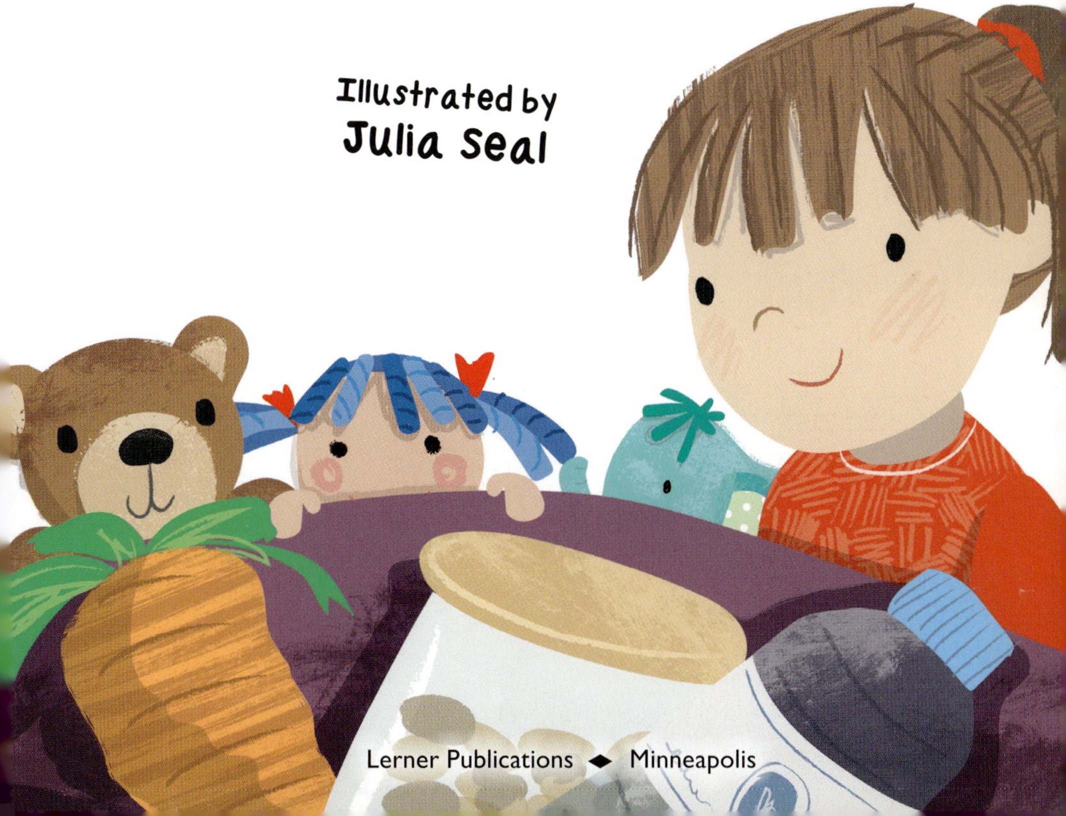

Lerner Publications ◆ Minneapolis

The Letter "T"

Trace the lowercase and uppercase letter with a finger. Sound out the letter.

Down, lift, cross

Down, lift, cross

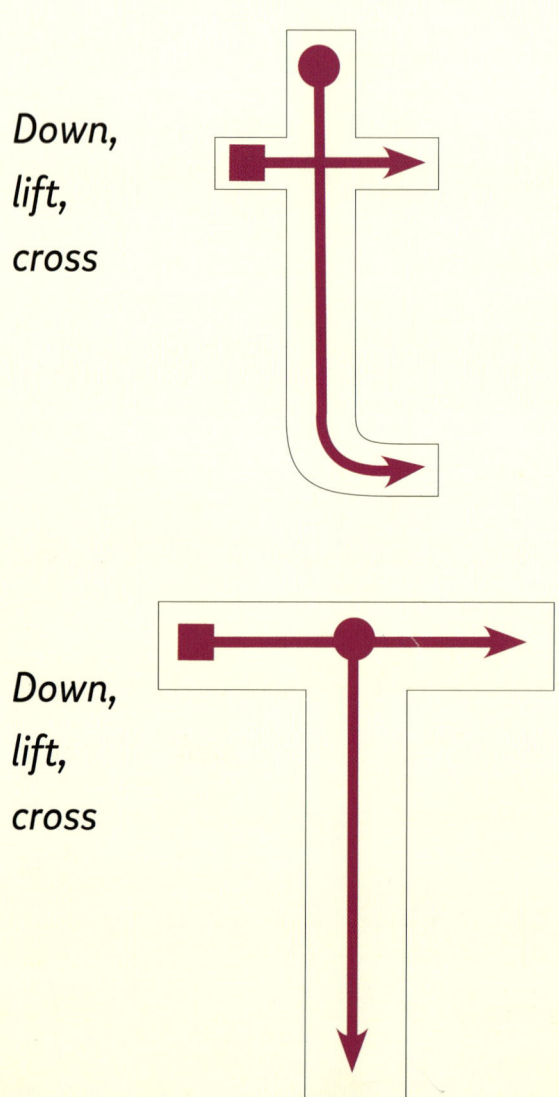

Some words to familiarize:

run   Nick   Nat

High-frequency words:
he   can   she

Tips for Reading *Tag!*

- Practice the words listed above before reading the story.
- If the reader struggles with any of the other words, ask them to look for sounds they know in the word. Encourage them to sound out the words and help them read the words if necessary.
- After reading the story, ask the reader who is tagged last.

Fun Activity

Have your own game of tag!

Tag!

Sam can run.

He can tag Tom.

Tom can run.

He can tag Nick.

Nick can run.

He can tag Sid.

Sid can run.

He can tag Nat.

Miss Neff tags Sam.

The Letter "G"

Trace the lowercase and uppercase letter with a finger. Sound out the letter.

Around,
up,
down,
around

Around,
up,
lift,
cross

Some words to familiarize:

carrot   drink   treat

High-frequency words:
a   put   in   the

Tips for Reading *In Pip's Bag*

- Practice the words listed above before reading the story.
- If the reader struggles with any of the other words, ask them to look for sounds they know in the word. Encourage them to sound out the words and help them read the words if necessary.
- After reading the story, ask the reader what Pip is packing her bag for.

Fun Activity

Make your own picnic and eat outside.

In Pip's Bag

Pip had a big bag.

Pip put nuts in the bag.

Pip put a carrot in the bag.

Pip put a drink in the bag.

Pip put a treat in the bag.

Pip had a picnic!

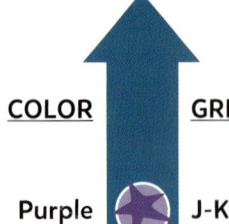

COLOR	GRL
Purple	J-K
Orange	H-J
Green	G-I
Blue	E-G
Yellow	C-E
Red	C-D
Pink	A-C

Leveled for Guided Reading

Early Bird Stories have been edited and leveled by leading educational consultants to correspond with guided reading levels. The levels are assigned by taking into account the content, language style, layout, and phonics used in each book.